The Princess and the Unicorn

From the Books of

Heather
Bull

The Princess and the Unicorn

By

Marika Hanbury Tenison

Illustrated by Ann Evans

GRANADA
London Toronto Sydney New York

Respectfully Dedicated
to
HER ROYAL HIGHNESS
PRINCESS MICHAEL OF KENT
This fairy tale
By the author Marika Hanbury Tenison

Published by Granada Publishing 1981

Granada Publishing Limited
Frogmore, St Albans, Herts AL2 2NF
and
36 Golden Square, London W1R 4AH
866 United Nations Plaza, New York, NY 10017, USA
117 York Street, Sydney, NSW 2000, Australia
100 Skyway Avenue, Rexdale, Ontario, M9W 3A6, Canada
61 Beach Road, Auckland, New Zealand

Hardback ISBN 0 246 11529 7
Paperback ISBN 0 583 30474 5

Printed in Singapore

Set in Baskerville

Granada ®
Granada Publishing ®

Chapter 1

*T*his is a story about something that happened a very, very long time ago. About something that happened when ladies wore long dresses sweeping to the ground, when they had hair so long they had to brush it a thousand times a day and braid it carefully in two plaits. The days when men, and even boys, fought battles from horseback and wounded each other with swords and lances.

But this is not a story about wars or battles. It is a true story of the love a Princess had for a milk white Unicorn and of the love he had for her.

The Princess lived in a land called Trevellia, a land of forests and mountains where the King and his family lived in a castle surrounded by a moat. Trevellia was not a big land. It had only two towns, ten villages, and only eleven thousand people lived there. They were happy people who farmed their sheep and spun and wove beautiful cloths which they sold to neighbouring countries. Their King was a fair and good ruler and his only sadness was that he had no son to rule Trevellia after he died. However, the King did have a very beautiful daughter and everyone hoped that one day she would marry a fine prince who would be able to follow in the good King's footsteps.

It was autumn. In the forest the great beech trees were turning from green to gold and copper, dropping their leaves like polished pennies on to the green velvety moss below.

Everywhere in the forest there was activity. The animals were busy making preparations for the long winter. The golden lions let their manes and coats grow long and shaggy as they looked for a cave that would be dry and warm for them to live in amongst the jumble of craggy rocks that rose up in the middle of the forest. The red squirrels jumped from tree to tree, collecting beech and hazel nuts. They stored them secretly in the hollow trunks of old dead trees. The spotted jumping deer scraped up the sweet-smelling pine needles under the fir trees and piled them into soft beds on the sheltered side of the large dark trees. Even the swift, bushy-tailed foxes were preparing for the winter by eating as much as they could so as not to get too hungry during the coming months when any food would be hard to find.

In the castle, the Royal family and the Royal household were also busy preparing for the winter. Over a hundred people lived there with the King, the Queen and the beautiful Princess. There were page boys and maids, hunters and soldiers, cooks and scullery boys, and even a Prime Minister to help the King govern Trevellia. Everyone would need food and warm clothing for the cold months ahead.

Each day the King and his hunters went out into the forest, coming back late in the evening with fresh game to be salted for the winter and stored in great wooden vats. In the kitchen cooks were pickling and preserving, packing apples into stone jars and making jam. The Queen spent much of her time in the stillroom, making her own secret recipe of elderberry cordial and watching over the wine making.

Throughout the whole land of Trevellia, everyone was busy. While they worked they sang for the summer had been long and the harvest had been good.

Everyone was busy and everyone was happy except for the Princess in the castle and the Unicorn in the forest. Neither of them had anything to do and both of them were unhappy.

The Princess was unhappy because she had no-one to talk to and no-one to play with. She could not go hunting with her father in the forest because she was a girl and girls didn't go hunting. When she went down to the kitchen and the preserving rooms, the Queen shooed her out, saying that she was in the way. The maids scowled at her, looking cross when she bumped against the jars of

9

rose petal jelly put to set in a cool place. Her own maid,
Sylvie, who usually talked and played with her, was busy
stirring jam. Even her old nurse was too busy to pay
attention to her. She was sewing the skins of the animals
the King had shot into thick heavy covers for the Royal
beds.

She wished that she had a brother or sister. She
wished that she was allowed to play with the children from
the village on the other side of the moat. But, because she
was a Princess, she could only give them a Royal wave
from the distance. Eventually she went for a walk alone in
the garden and ran under the trees trying to catch the
copper leaves as they drifted down from the branches. She
knew that if you catch a falling leaf before it touches the
ground you can make a wish and the wish will come true.
But every time that the Princess was sure she had a leaf in
her hands a little breeze whisked it away and she was left
with nothing.

Deep in the forest, the Unicorn was also unhappy.
Being the only Unicorn in the forest, he had no-one to
build a home with. The other animals who usually talked
to him about this and that were far too busy to spend any

time with him. None of them ever suggested that he
might like to share their homes for the winter. He had his
own home high on the top of a mountain far in the forest
and he spent all the day by himself becoming more and
more lonely and sad. His pure white coat and his beard
had grown long and silky for the winter and his mane fell
gracefully down his neck. His tail almost brushed the
ground, it was so long. When he trotted through the
forest paths, his tail floated out behind him like a white
silk banner. He carried his head very high so that

11

everyone could see his beautiful straight white horn. It was so white and so polished that it looked like moonshine. But his beauty was wasted as nobody looked at him.

Sometimes the Unicorn would hear the sound of the King's hunting horn in the distance and the baying of the Royal hounds. Then he would gallop deeper into the forest to the safety of the thick trees.

One day, the Unicorn did not run to hide when he first heard the sound of the hunt. He was so bored that he thought he would stay and see what they were like, these hunters that all the animals in the forest feared so much.

It was nearly evening when the Unicorn heard the horn. He was having a drink at one of the forest pools, amusing himself by dipping the tip of his horn into the water and then shaking it so that the drops of water scattered about like crystal jewels. Suddenly, he heard one sharp clear note of the hunting horn, not very far away. A panting stag raced past him, leaping over the pool with a bound, shouting as he disappeared amongst the trees, 'flee, flee for your life!' But the Unicorn did not flee. Instead he ran swiftly towards a high crag. He leapt up and up, from rock to rock and then stood still on the top, knowing that the hunt would pass below him.

Soon he saw them. The hounds in front, baying; then came the King, a fine sight on his coal black horse. He wore a long scarlet cloak with an edging of gold. His saddle was made of silver and he had a golden eagle's feather in his hat. Behind him rode the chief hunters, dressed in yellow, with bows slung over their shoulders and hooded falcons on their wrists. At the back were the huntsmen with sharp knives tucked in their leather belts, and curled hunting horns of shining copper hanging by their sides. The Unicorn gazed down in wonder.

At the edge of the pool the hounds lost the scent. The King put up his hand for the huntsmen to stop their horses and looked all around for signs of the deer.

Looking up, he saw the Unicorn poised on the high crag, outlined against the sky standing like a statue. At first he thought he must be dreaming, but one of the huntsmen, seeing the King staring so hard, turned to look too and, on catching sight of the Unicorn, gave a loud cry.

'Unicorn, Unicorn', echoed through the forest.

All was at once in confusion.

The huntsmen called the hounds and set them to follow the scent of the Unicorn. The King galloped towards the crag with the hunters following closely behind him. For a moment, the Unicorn watched them. Then, realising his danger, he swiftly fled down the far side of the crag. By the time the huntsmen had reached the top, the Unicorn was far away in the safety of the dark forest. Although the hounds picked up his scent, and the hunters urged their tired horses into a gallop, they caught only a glimpse of the Unicorn in the distance before the sun went down behind the hill and it grew dark.

When the forest was silent again, the Unicorn lay down to rest by a stream. His heart was thudding, but it had been the most exciting thing that had ever happened to him and he was proud to know that he was so much fleeter than all the Royal hunters.

The ground by the stream was soft and still warm from the day's sunshine. Buttercups and autumn crocuses filled the air with a sweet perfume. Soon the Unicorn fell asleep.

Chapter 2

*I*n the castle, the Princess waited in her room for the hunters to return. Her room was high at the top of the western tower of the castle with a window that looked out over the gardens and the moat towards the river and the forest. Her bed was large and soft with a swansdown mattress and covered with soft fur rugs. Curtains of woven tapestry hung round the bed. On the walls were silver sconces holding candles to light the room at night.

The walls of the castle were so thick that the windowsill was a metre wide. It was here that the Princess, kneeling on a cushion of peacock blue silk, watched for the King to come home.

The hunters rode into the courtyard. Grooms ran forward to help the King from his horse. The hounds bayed. The game they had killed during the day was brought in and the falcons were taken off to their perches.

At last, the King strode into the Great Hall and stood warming himself by the huge fire of blazing apple logs, drinking a flagon of ale. A page boy came to pull off his hunting boots. The Queen and the Princess were by his side, and the Prime Minister and the other most important members of the Royal household stood around about him eager to hear of the day's hunting.

The King told them of how he had seen the Unicorn and they were as excited as the King himself. Everyone knew what the capture of a Unicorn meant. They knew that the Unicorn is one of the most magical and rarest animals on this earth. Deadly liquid poured into a cup made from the horn of the Unicorn will turn instantly to the purest of wines; even to touch poison with the tip of his horn will make the liquid free from anything that is harmful.

Now the King of Trevellia was a good King and much loved by his people, but like all Kings he had enemies. Men who would like to see him killed so that they might seize his land and his castle for themselves. Enemies that might try to poison his wine. So it was no wonder that the King, his hunters and the whole of the

Royal household were excited beyond words that evening at the thought of the capture of the Unicorn and of the drinking cup that could be made for the King from the magical Unicorn's horn.

The Princess asked her father again and again to describe the Unicorn to her. The King told her how he

was the fastest and fleetest animal he had ever seen; how his carriage and bearing was like that of a Monarch; how it was almost impossible to put into words his infinite grace and purity.

Tarquin, the chief huntsman, said that the Unicorn was so white that he was almost blinded when he saw him standing proudly on the top of the crag. Marcus, the falcon keeper, said that his horn was so long and so pointed that it resembled a silver sword. Sebastian, the youngest of the hunters, swore that his mane and tail were like the finest, purest, silk blowing in the wind.

Talk went on, throughout the long evening meal, of the Unicorn and the plans for his capture, until the King commanded them all to go early to bed so as to be fresh for the hunt next day.

Chapter 3

*N*ext morning, before the sun had properly risen in the East, the King and the hunters left the castle. The Princess rode with her father as far as the edge of the forest on her brown and white dappled horse, Persimmon. There she wished the hunters luck and stayed waving as they disappeared from view, round a curve of the path, into the darkness of the forest. She wished so much that she could have ridden with them and seen the beautiful Unicorn.

In the forest, the King led the hunters straight to the crag where they had first seen the Unicorn. The hounds were unleashed to pick up his scent. The huntsmen placed arrows in their bows and raised their hunting horns.

The Unicorn was still in the dell beside the stream where he had spent the night. He was breakfasting on tender blades of grass and peony leaves and was practising leaping over the stream. He was so busy that the hunters were almost upon him before he heard the baying of the hounds and the long notes of their copper horns.

The hunters cheered. The hounds bayed louder and the King waved his feathered cap in the air, crying 'Onward! Onward!'

Swift as an arrow from a bow, the Unicorn leapt forward, over the stream once more, to the safety of the trees. Faster and faster he ran, a streak of silver through the pine trees. Jumping over fallen logs, racing through groves of twisted oak leaves. He twisted and turned to get away from the hunt, stopping for a quick drink at a pool as the baying of the hounds grew fainter. Then on he raced again as the hounds drew close once more. Down into the valleys where the myrtle grew. Deeper and deeper into the forest where the trees were so close together their branches met and entwined.

For a long time the Unicorn did not tire. He galloped smoothly, swiftly, sure of foot, and with an unerring knowledge of the great forest where he had spent his life. But, towards afternoon, he found his heart was thudding painfully. He rested for a moment in a grove of silver cypress trees. Under the flat, spreading branches, it was refreshingly cool. His breath stopped coming in painful gasps. When the hunt came nearer, he was rested and sped off again.

All through the day the chase went on. When the sun began to set they had reached a place so deep in the heart of the forest that even the oldest of the hunters had never been there before. A strange and magical valley that the Unicorn knew well, where ancient, gnarled, distorted trees grew from cracks in grey boulders and dipped their branches into a bubbling, tumbling river. At the head of this valley, the river fell from the top of a small, rocky mountain in a swift, sparkling waterfall. This mountain was the Unicorn's haunt. His home was on the top where sweet-scented juniper trees grew in a circle round a glade of the softest emerald green moss, buttoned with daisies. In the centre of the glade was a deep, clear pool fed by a ribbon of the purest spring water.

When the King reached this enchanted valley, it was too dark to see the mountain. The moon was only just rising and all he could see was the river and the outlines of the ancient trees. He called the hunters around him and they agreed that the chase must be given up for the day. The hunters blew their horns to call the hounds and they turned southwards towards home.

As they left the strange valley, the King looked back and saw what looked to him like a vision. In the sky, for the King could not see the outline of the mountain in the darkness, he caught a glimpse of the Unicorn's horn, glinting in the light of the rising moon. A pointed, silver spiral. Magical, breathtaking and beautiful.

Wearily the hunters rode the long journey back to the castle. Back through the cypress glades, the oak trees and the pine forest. The horses stumbled with fatigue. The hounds slunk with their tails between their legs, starting as night owls hooted and glided on silent wings across their path. The forest was black and the moon gave

the only light to guide their way. It was very late when they reached the moat and the welcoming gates of the castle.

That night there was no joking and drinking of toasts. No-one dared laugh, for the King was in a black and sombre mood. All day had been spent in the pursuit of the Unicorn. No game had been killed for the winter and at least five horses and three hounds had been badly lamed during the chase.

When the meal was over, the King rose and spoke gravely.

'It is of the greatest importance to our country that we should capture the Unicorn,' he said. 'We have tried to hunt it and we have failed. Very soon the winter will be upon us and we have little time left. It is our Royal Command that you should all think of some means of capturing this wondrous beast. The person who provides the way to the capture of the Unicorn will be rewarded with the granting of any request he should make to us.'

None could think of any answer to the problem. Even the Princess, who normally had a lot to say, was silent. Even the Prime Minister, the wisest man in Trevellia, could not think of a solution to the problem and merely coughed and tut-tutted into his long grey beard. At last, the Princess's old nurse rose from her place at the lowest end of the table. She was very old and when she walked she was bent like a hoop. Slowly she went up to the King and curtsied.

'Please, Sire,' she said in her cracked, thin, voice that was little more than a whisper. 'When I was a girl, my grandmother told me that the only way a Unicorn could ever be caught was by a young and beautiful girl, and that in the old days young men were dressed up as girls, powdered and scented and taken out into the

forests. The Unicorn would come up to them and allow himself to be captured.'

The Princess listened in great excitement. She was the one who could capture the Unicorn. After all, she was a girl. She was young and everyone said she was beautiful. She knew without a shadow of doubt that if she went into the forest the Unicorn would come to her.

She pleaded with the King but he would not listen. He insisted that the forest was no place for a Princess. She might get hurt. She was the only child he had and he was not going to risk her life.

The Princess begged and cried but the King would not change his mind. Together with his Prime Minister and the chief of the huntsmen, Tarquin, he withdrew into his Council. Here they made plans to lure the Unicorn in the way that the old nurse had suggested by dressing up one of the Royal page boys to look like a girl and taking him into the forest the next day.

They chose a boy called Bertrand who had a fair, handsome face and a slight, girlish build. Bertrand was delighted. It would be an exciting day and at the end of it he would be able to claim a reward from the King. Already he could think of many things to ask for.

When the Princess went to bed that night, she cried and cried. Her maid, Sylvie, helped her to undress, begging the Princess to be more cheerful, but the Princess sent her away. When the old nurse came to draw the tapestry curtains round the bed and to snuff out the candles, the Princess was still crying. The old woman leant over the bed and whispered to her, 'Calm yourself, my child. Tomorrow they will fail again, and the very next day you will have your chance.'

She stroked the Princess's soft, golden hair with her hand and sang a gentle song until the girl fell asleep, dreaming of the dark forest and the pure white Unicorn.

Chapter 4

*T*he next day was Saturday and the sun rose brightly over Trevellia. But, far in the distance, over the border in the mountainous country of Serba, the snow clouds were building up. Thick white masses of cloud hung low over the mountain peaks slowly moving southwards. In a day or two, the slopes of Serba would be two metres thick in snow and the fast-flowing rivers would freeze solid. Soon the snows would reach Trevellia and there would be no more hunting until spring.

The Princess breakfasted hurriedly in bed. Having breakfast in bed was another thing she didn't like about being a Princess. Crumbs dropped inside her nightgown and tickled and she never felt so hungry lying down, but the old nurse insisted that all princesses had breakfast in bed and that was that.

Impatiently, the Princess stood first on one foot and then the other while Sylvie dressed her. This morning it all seemed to take much longer than usual. Petticoats, her dress, her silken stockings and slippers, and at last her

hair which had to be brushed and brushed and finally bound up with golden cords and braided tightly around her head. At last she was ready and flew down the stone steps to the King's Council Chamber where the page boy, Bertrand, was being dressed up in girl's clothing.

Bertrand was nearly ready by the time she got there, looking so like a girl that the Princess could not help giggling a little at the change. Gone was a page boy who had always been getting into mischief and who spent all the time he could on horseback, practising in the jousting paddock, who, bruised and muddied from countless falls, would race up to the castle to change and be ready to wait on the King at the dining table. In his place stood a pretty, demure girl. His hair was hidden by a tall white hat with a silk scarf of scarlet floating from the top. He wore a dress of scarlet wool with long wide sleeves and a train that trailed on the ground hiding his leather hunting boots. They had not been able to find any girl's slippers large enough to fit him. The Queen's own maid had painted his lips with the juice from red geranium petals and had lightly brushed his cheeks with a layer of the finest white powder.

The other page boys thought it was the greatest joke and, when Bertrand was ready, they sprinkled him with sweet smelling scent, a mixture of the perfume of roses and carnations and scampered round the poor boy, teasing him unmercifully. He blushed in embarrassment and looked more like a pretty girl than ever. He was greatly relieved when the King gave the order for the hunt to move off. The Queen herself arranged the folds of his dress so as to hide his leather boots, pinning the skirt securely to the richly woven trappings of his saddle. Bertrand felt very important.

The Princess ran upstairs to watch from the window seat in her room as the riders set off towards the forest.

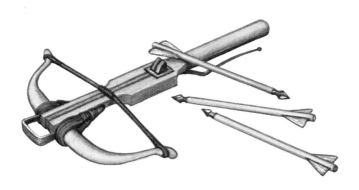

It was a gay and colourful sight as the hunters wound their way down the hill, across the drawbridge, over the moat and towards the river. The sun glinted on the King's silver saddle; the horses shone from daily grooming and the hunters' uniforms made a moving pattern beside the blue ribbon of the wide river.

In the castle they waited with as much patience as they could for the evening when the hunters would return.

In the forest, animals scurried swiftly away to their secret hiding places at the approaching sound of the huntsmen. They were not to know that today the King was hunting only one animal, the legendary Unicorn.

The Unicorn heard them too. His ears pricked forward but he was not worried. He knew that he was

faster than their horses, fleeter than their hounds and that he could outrun them at any time.

It was mid-day before the hunt came near to the place where they had last seen the Unicorn the night before. Here the King commanded Bertrand to dismount from his horse and to sit close to the edge of the water. A huntsman led his horse away.

The King and the chief hunter also dismounted and went to hide themselves amongst the trees, not too far from Bertrand so that they could hear should he call out. The rest of the huntsmen, the horses and the hounds went back into the forest blowing their horns and shouting so that the Unicorn would think they were hunting other game.

The Unicorn had been watching the huntsmen from a safe distance. He saw the maiden and was fascinated by her beauty, by the richness of her gown and by the pale whiteness of her skin.

Keeping hidden amongst the trees, following beside the hunters, and gazing on this vision, he watched the maiden dismount and then saw the hunters go away.

The Unicorn longed to go nearer to the maiden. The wind blew her sweet scent towards him, a haunting, lingering scent that made him feel almost faint with desire to touch her soft skin and to lay his head on the gentle folds of her long dress. Slowly, step by step, he moved towards Bertrand. Every sense in his body trembled. His bones felt weak.

The boy looked up and stretched out his arm towards the beast. From his hiding place, the King watched, holding his breath in excitement, praying that the animal would fall into his trap.

Seen this close, the Unicorn was even more beautiful than the King believed possible. His whiteness

was the silver whiteness of the stars. His horn like polished ivory. His cloven hooves were as dainty as a child's foot and his eyes held the softness of a doe in spring.

When the Unicorn was almost close enough for Bertrand to touch him, the boy rose to his feet and stretched out his hand to place it on the Unicorn's horn. As he moved, the train of the scarlet dress fell back and the leather hunting boots showed clearly below the hem of his skirt. At once, the Unicorn realised he had been tricked. Beneath the powerful smell of perfume, he smelt the unmistakeable scent of MAN. He reared up, his horn ripping through the wide sleeve of the red dress. Tensing all his muscles, he gave a bound that took him two metres away from the boy and he was free, racing for the safety of the trees, fleeing through the forest that he knew so well.

The King gave a shout of warning. The chief hunter loosed an arrow from his bow that grazed past the Unicorn's right shoulder as he ran. The huntsmen unleashed the hounds and unhooded their falcons, but it was too late. The Unicorn was free.

Once more, they returned to the castle empty handed.

Chapter 5

Bertrand had failed. The nurse's words came true and the Princess had her wish. On the next day, Sunday, she rode beside her father into the forest.

The King was a religious man. Normally, he would not have dreamt of hunting on Sunday, but the snow clouds over Serba were creeping nearer, already a messenger had arrived to say that it was snowing heavily there, and there was no time to lose before the winter closed in.

Before they left the castle, the Priest blessed the whole party. The Queen fondly kissed her daughter and, at the last minute, unloosed the gold braids that bound up her hair so that it flowed down over her shoulders, shining in the sunlight, the colour of ripe corn in summer. She was beautiful. Her skin had the unblemished fairness of youth and her cheeks glowed softly pink without the aid of powder or rouge. Her figure was perfectly slender, enhanced by the gown she wore of palest blue silk with a girdle of silver strands. Her beauty was breathtaking.

As they entered the forest, the Princess felt a shiver of fear run through her. Everywhere there seemed to be an air of strange excitement, of expectancy. The trees were taller and darker than she had imagined. Strange noises in the undergrowth made her glance nervously from side to side, and a harsh wind made her draw her cloak of ermine more closely around her.

But soon the reassurance of her father beside her made her forget her fright and the Princess began to look around her at the strange beauties of the forest. Once, she caught a glimpse of a noble lion, amber eyes glowing through the trees. In the sky, a golden eagle circled, moving lazily until something caught his sharp eye and he plummeted down to earth.

When they reached the pool deep in the forest, the King left his hunters and went on alone with his daughter. It was so dark and silent that the Princess grew frightened again. The twisted trees seemed to take on strange shapes. A slight wind moved without noise through the leaves, making them dance, stirring the strands of grey lichen that hung from the tree trunks and branches. Even the horses seemed nervous, snorting through their nostrils in the way horses do when they are ill at ease.

They came at last to the place the King had chosen for the capture of the Unicorn. Wild flowers glowed like many-coloured jewels on a velvet background of moss. Logwood trailed its rosy branches into a pool of water, breaking the reflection of the clear sky above. It was a place of mystery and magic.

The Princess got down from her horse, took off her cloak and spread it on the ground. The King kissed her gravely and presently left her sitting alone on her cloak by the water's edge.

It was quiet by the water. To break the strange silence the Princess began to sing a lullaby, one of the songs that the old nurse had so often sung to send her to sleep. It was her singing that lured the Unicorn down from his haunt towards her.

He had been watching the progress of the hunters from his haunt on the top of his mountain. He caught glimpses of the Princess as they rode through the forest and was angry that they were attempting to trick him again. When the King left the Princess alone by the stream, he had laughed to himself that they should believe him to be so easily taken in.

Yet, now that he could see the Princess more clearly, the Unicorn found it hard to believe that this vision was a man in maiden's disguise. Everything about her was perfection and the foot that peeped from beneath the silken hem of her dress was shod in the daintiest of golden slippers.

When the Princess began to sing, the Unicorn knew without doubt that this was no trick. Here was the real maiden of his dreams. Her voice was soft and tender. The words floated upwards towards him, flooding him with a sense of unbelievable happiness and peace. He descended the mountainside towards her.

The nearer he came to her, the more beautiful she seemed. His pace quickened and soon he reached the edge of the clearing by the stream. It was at this moment that the Princess saw him. The words of her song died on her lips as she gazed in wonder at his beauty and grace. For a moment she closed her eyes, his whiteness dazzling her. The Unicorn, her Unicorn, was so perfect, so unbelievably magical, that the very air around her seemed touched with enchantment, and she gasped with wonder.

40

Nearer and nearer he came to where she sat. Softly she whispered to him, 'My Unicorn, my perfect milk white Unicorn.' When he was close beside her, so close that she could feel the very warmth of his breath, she lifted her hand to touch the softness of his coat, to caress the silkiness of his mane. With the softest of sighs, he dropped his head. Kneeling down beside her, he placed his head on the welcome softness of her lap.

For a long time, the Princess and the Unicorn stayed together, quite still, with just her hand moving gently to caress his forehead, both content to be together.

At last, she rose. Undoing the silver cord from around her waist, she placed it round the Unicorn's neck and led him away from the stream, towards her father, the King. He followed meekly beside her as though bound by a cord far stronger than the silver threads around his neck.

The King was intensely moved by the magic and
the wonder of the moment. He said nothing but kissed his
daughter once more. Together the three of them walked
slowly back towards the hunters and the path to the castle.

Chapter 6

*T*he hunters were restless. They had waited for a long time. It was beginning to get really cold and they were worried about the safety of their beloved King and Princess.

Just as the Chief Hunter was thinking he should take a few men to look for the King, he saw them coming towards him. The King and the Princess with the Unicorn between them led by a cord of silver. It was a moment that they would never forget. Their Princess, more beautiful, more golden than they had ever seen her, with, beside her, the perfection and the whiteness of the Unicorn. The hunters rubbed their eyes, taking a minute or two to understand that what they saw was true.

The moment ended. They forgot the beauty and rushed forward with their knives to cut off the Unicorn's head. Shouting in their harsh, loud voices.

The Unicorn backed away, trembling with fear. He strained against the cord around his neck and would have broken free but for the Princess's soft hand on his neck. The King raised his hand for order and the hunters fell back, silent once more.

Now the King was a wise man, but for once he was at a loss to know what to do for the best. The Unicorn was so wondrous it seemed a crime to kill him or to cut off his horn. On the other hand, the magical qualities of his horn were of the utmost value.

Then the Princess said, 'Father, the Unicorn is mine. You made a promise that whoever helped you to capture him would be granted any request they named. My request is that the Unicorn should be mine.'

'Cut off his horn. Kill the Unicorn,' murmured the hunters. 'Make a drinking flagon from the magic horn to protect our King from poison.'

Angrily, the Princess turned on them. 'You men are foolish and short-sighted. Kill the Unicorn and you will be left with nothing but a cup. Let him live and every time the King has cause to drink, the Unicorn can dip his horn into my father's cup to test its purity.'

The hunters shuffled their feet, looking down at the ground. But the King was delighted with his daughter. 'My child.' he said, 'you are old beyond your years, and wiser than your father. You shall indeed keep the Unicorn and we will return rejoicing that God has seen fit to grant us this marvellous gift.'

So they rode homewards through the forest. The Princess in front with her father, the Unicorn close beside her, his head held high, his polished horn shining in the evening sun.

At the gates of the castle, the villagers had gathered to watch for the return of the Princess and the hunting party. When they saw the Unicorn, they cheered again and again, rushing forward to touch the hem of the Princess's skirt as she passed them.

Only Bertrand, the page boy, did not cheer with the rest. He had failed where the Princess, only a girl, had succeeded. He felt humiliated and bitter that she who already had everything had been the one to have a request granted by the King. He stayed away from the celebrations, sulking in his room.

That evening, the castle rang with laughter and singing. A feast had been quickly prepared, and the Princess, sitting on the left hand of the King, had the Unicorn beside her. Although the strangeness of being under a roof and not the star-sown sky made him tremble, the nearness of the Princess comforted him. He kept his head raised proudly.

When the King's goblet was filled with wine, the Princess rose to her feet. Taking the Unicorn's horn gently in her hand, she guided it until the very tip dipped into the goblet. It seemed that the wine clouded over for a moment. Then it took on an extra purity. The drops that scattered from the tip of the Unicorn's horn sparkled in the candlelight like the finest of rubies. In complete silence, the King raised his glass, draining it in one draught.

The cheering that followed swelled up and up. The banners of the King's armies that hung overhead fluttered and swung as though in a strong breeze.

The Princess was happy but tired. So, excusing herself to the King and Queen, she led the Unicorn up the stone steps to her room in the western tower of the castle.

The old nurse had arranged a bed of furs and silk for the Unicorn to lie on. In the soft glow of the lamplight, the Princess could just see him lying at the foot of her bed. She whispered, 'Goodnight, my dearest pure white Unicorn.' He raised his head and, looking across to her, his dark eyes answered, 'Goodnight, my dearest fair Princess.'

Chapter 7

*T*he next morning, it began to snow. In the castle and every house throughout Trevellia last minute preparations were being made for winter. Everywhere there was fuss and flurry. The last of the meat was salted. The Royal goats and sheep were herded into the courtyard. Extra cartloads of firewood were hauled up the hill, the horses' feet already slipping as the snow began to freeze on the ground. The King held his last conference of the year and promised that the first day of spring would be a special holiday to be known as the Day of the Unicorn.

The Princess was the happiest person in the whole land. As usual, she had breakfast in bed. But this time the Unicorn was there to share it with her. He nibbled daintily at a piece of toast and seemed delighted with a bowl of warmed milk.

When the maid, Sylvie, had combed the Princess's golden hair and dressed her in a dress of green, the

Princess took her own brush and combed the Unicorn's mane and the beard under his chin. She perfumed him with a scent of roses and polished his horn with a silk cloth. Then she placed a bracelet of sapphires over the shining horn. Lifting up her mirror of beaten silver, she showed him the reflection of his beauty. In gratitude, he placed his front hooves on her lap and thanked her with the look in his soft, deep eyes.

During the morning, they watched the slow, lazy snowflakes falling in their millions, covering the ground with a blanket of whiteness. The snow was white and sparkling but not so white as the coat and mane of the Unicorn.

The Princess asked the Royal goldsmith to make a collar and a thin chain of gold to go round the Unicorn's neck. The collar was to be in the shape of a crown, light as

a feather. The chain to lead him by was to be studded with pearls.

And so the winter came. It snowed every day and night for three weeks. Every day, the Princess loved the Unicorn more. He was never from her side. She combed him and brushed him, walked with him along the wide top of the castle walls where the snow had been swept away. She dressed him in the finest of her jewels. She fed him only the tastiest titbits from the dining table, and every mealtime she led him to her father's cup where he would touch the King's wine with the tip of his horn to make sure it was unpoisoned and pure. After the Unicorn had touched the wine, the King said that it took on a coolness and a mellowness such as he had never before tasted in the castle or anywhere else.

The Unicorn was happy too, for he loved the Princess. Sometimes he longed to gallop as fast as he could for miles and miles, but he knew that the forest would be thick with snow and very very cold and he liked the warmth and comfort of the castle. When he was restless, the Princess would stroke his soft head and sing to him until his doe-like eyes once more filled with contentment.

The maids in the castle had little to do during these dark winter days so the Queen instructed them to weave a tapestry for the Princess. It would hang behind her bed when it was finished and was to be a picture of all the things that she knew and loved: the river and the castle, all the animals of the forest and her Unicorn, lying in a green glade by a forest pool surrounded by flowers.

The King commanded that a painter should paint a picture of the Princess and the Unicorn. It was to show the Unicorn resting his head on her lap, and the Princess holding up her silver hand mirror to show the reflection of his beauty. Every afternoon they posed for the painting. The Princess sang her songs and outside the wind swept across the valley and through the great forest.

On Christmas Day, there was a great feast at the castle. Everyone was there from the lowest servant girl upwards. They ate, sang and danced until morning and the Princess was beautiful in a new dress of the palest silvery pink embroidered with pearls. Her hair was so brushed, so shining that it looked like a halo around her delicate face. From the top of the centre table she smiled her sweet smile at everyone, sitting all the evening with her arm around the neck of her pure white Unicorn.

Only Bertrand, the page boy, did not dance or sing like the others. He sat by himself, sulky and morose, eaten up with jealousy for the beauty, the Royal birth, and the riches of the Princess. Above all for her Unicorn which should by rights, he felt, have been his prize.

Chapter 8

*J*anuary passed, February passed. Quite suddenly, winter ended. The sun shone all day. The snow began to melt. Icicles disappeared into drops of water. In the castle, the maids and page boys went about their work singing and humming.

In the forest, the lion walked in the sunshine, easing his cramped limbs. The squirrels woke. The badgers yawned and stretched. The hedgehogs uncurled. Birds appeared from nowhere, singing at the tops of their voices. The red fox discovered a tiny yellow jonquil pushing its way bravely through the remains of the snow.

Spring was in the air, the sky, on the ground, everywhere.

The castle gates were thrown open and the King, remembering his promise, sent messengers to the towns and villages to declare the first day of spring a public holiday: 'The Day of the Unicorn'. Barrels of wine from the castle were put in the squares and meeting places and a present of one pound of salted meat was given to every Trevellian over eighty years old. In every home throughout the land toasts were drunk and cheers raised to the glory of their beautiful Princess and her Unicorn.

One day, a messenger arrived at the castle bearing a letter to the King of Trevellia from the King of Serba. It said that his second son, Prince Tallyrand, was on his way to pay his respects to the King and the people of Trevellia, sent by his father to ask for the hand of the Princess of Trevellia in marriage.

Preparations were begun immediately for the visit. The Prince was to arrive the next day and there was no time to be lost. Everyone was delighted because as a husband for the Princess, and as 'a future King of Trevellia, the young Prince Tallyrand was suitable in every way. He was said to have the dark, handsome looks of his father, and to have a kindness and sensibility amazing in one so young.

Only the Princess was not excited by the forthcoming visit. She had no wish to be married. She was completely happy and content with the company of her milk white Unicorn, and took no interest in the arrangements.

When the young Prince Tallyrand arrived the next afternoon, the Princess was in her room gazing at the picture of herself with her Unicorn. She heard, from far below, the trumpets heralding the arrival of the guests. From her window, she looked down and saw the procession riding through the scarlet-coated guard of honour up to the castle. For the first time, she laid eyes on Prince Tallyrand.

52

She had never seen a man so handsome and so fine. He was bare-headed, and his black hair shone like a raven's wing, blacker than the cloak of velvet that swung from his shoulders. Black too was his charger, larger than any horse in the castle, groomed to shining ebony. And black also were the emblems of the banners that the Prince's servants carried behind him, the black eagle of Serba.

But the Prince's eyes were clear blue. As he passed beneath the arch of the courtyard, he chanced to look upwards. Seeing the Princess at her window, he stopped his horse. They gazed at one another, and in that quick moment fell in love.

The Princess forgot the painting, forgot even the Unicorn lying in a corner of the room. Calling her maid, she spent the next hour preparing herself for the banquet that evening, putting on her very finest dress.

When at last she was ready the company were assembled in the dining hall and she walked in silence, the

Unicorn beside her, to where her place was laid between her father and the Prince.

When the Princess entered the hall, the Prince was discussing military matters with the King. But when he saw her he became silent, unable to keep his eyes off her as she walked towards him. She was so lovely, so fair and beautiful, dressed in a flowing gown of silver, her golden hair caught back with a deep red camellia, her only jewellery a ruby, hung on a golden chain around her neck. Beside her walked the pure white Unicorn whose magic horn would test the King's wine for poison and impurity.

The Prince rose to his feet and, taking the Princess's small, delicate hand in his strong one, he kissed it, and placed upon her finger a ring of gold and sapphires.

Later after dinner, when they danced together, the King and Queen rejoiced to see how quickly and how much they loved each other.

Then the engagement of the Royal couple was announced, the bells of Trevellia rang throughout the land, the messengers of good tidings and goodwill sped between the lands of Serba and Trevellia.

Chapter 9

*D*uring the days that preceded their wedding day, Prince Tallyrand and the Princess spent almost all their time together. They walked in the gardens and kissed beneath the blossoming arches of the almond trees. They rode side by side along the banks of the wide river, through the fields of growing corn. In the evenings they danced by candlelight in the Great Hall of the castle.

The Unicorn was forgotten.

Even when the young Prince went hunting with the King, the Princess was occupied being measured for her wedding dress. She could find no time to take the Unicorn for walks, to brush his pure white mane or to sing to him. Most of the time, she left him chained to a gold ring in the wall of her room, only leading him down the staircase to the hall when it was time for him to dip his horn into the King's goblet.

Each day the Unicorn grew more lonely and sad. His eyes became dark with suffering and heartbreak. His coat grew dull. As he looked down through the window towards the woods, he longed for the freedom of the forest and his haunt on the mountain top. He longed for the sound of fresh, running water and the remembered scent of juniper berries in the springtime. But he was held a prisoner, bound by a golden crown and chain.

Sometimes the old nurse would come and sit by him, stroking his head and singing the songs the Princess had once sung.

Once or twice, the page boy, Bertrand would sneak into the room and gaze with hatred and envy at the Unicorn and his magical horn. Then the Unicorn would be frightened and would back away knowing that there was evil in the boy's heart.

Ever since the day when Bertrand had been dressed as a girl and had failed to capture the Unicorn, the other page boys had teased him and scoffed at him. Forgotten was his jousting, his joy in riding an untamed or difficult horse. He longed only for power and riches. Realising that he would never achieve these in Trevellia, he had decided to run away and seek his fortune in some country far away. To do this, he needed money. So he made a plan. He would cut off the magical horn of the Unicorn and take it to a place where he knew he could sell it for a large sum of money.

On the eve of the wedding of Prince Tallyrand to the Princess of Trevellia, Bertrand got his chance. The Prince and Princess were out walking together in the garden. The maid, Sylvie, was in the sewing room. The rest of the household were busy with preparations for the great day.

Stealthily, Bertrand crept into the Princess's room. With his hunting knife unsheathed, he crept noiselessly across the room towards the Unicorn. He did not see the old nurse sleeping in a corner waiting for the Princess to return from her walk.

56

Reaching the Unicorn, he seized the magic horn
in one hand and began to cut it with his knife. The
Unicorn struggled, but Bertrand was as strong as a young
ox and the Unicorn was chained to the golden ring in the
wall.

Too late, the nurse awoke and screamed out.

Too late, the huntsman, Tarquin, heard the old nurse scream and ran to aid her, from the courtyard below.

The horn of the Unicorn was cut. In his hand, Bertrand held it. From its jagged end sprang beads of scarlet blood and blood ran down the white face of the wounded Unicorn.

In his haste to get away, Bertrand dropped the horn and ran empty handed from the room towards the stairs. Although the guards had been alerted, the boy escaped, and fled from the land across the border, never to be heard of again.

In the garden, the Princess had heard the commotion. A feeling of fear came over her as she ran to her room in the castle. There she saw her Unicorn with his eyes closed and his head bleeding from the wound where once the whiteness of his horn had sprung. Beside him, on the floor, lay the horn.

With a cry, the Princess was on her knees beside him, cradling his head in her lap as the old nurse rubbed healing salve into his wound. Slowly, with the longest of sighs, the Unicorn opened his soft, doe-like brown eyes, and seeing his Princess beside him, cried, but not in sorrow, in joy, because she loved him once more. And his pain was eased.

The Princess dried his tears with the golden tresses of her hair. She cried with him and together their tears mingled. The golden hair and the milky white mane entwined as they laid their heads together.

She sang the songs that the Unicorn had loved to hear, lullabies that soothed him finally into a deep, healing sleep, as she stroked his forehead and ran her gentle fingers down the whiteness of his neck. At last,

when the moon had risen, when the stars began to shine, the Princess too fell asleep, her Unicorn's head still cradled in her lap, her arm still around his neck.

Early in the morning, so early that the moon had not yet left the sky and the sun had not yet risen, the Princess awoke.

She looked upon a miracle.

During the short hours of darkness, the wound of the Unicorn had healed. Where his horn had been severed, a new horn had arisen. A horn, if anything, more silvery and more shining white than before. Only the drops of blood he had shed over her dress convinced the Princess that she had not been dreaming. His coat had taken on that almost unbelievable gleam of whiteness once again and her Unicorn was pure once more.

Then the Princess knew the time had come for her to take the Unicorn back into the forest where he belonged. Now her father, the King, could make a drinking cup from the Unicorn's horn, and he would be free to roam once more through his Kingdom.

Gently she woke him. Together, for the last time, they left her room, left the castle and walked through the gardens of the castle to the river.

Deeper and deeper into the forest they went, side by side. It seemed no time at all before they reached the stream where she had first placed her girdle of silver around his neck. In this place they said goodbye. Taking off the single perfect ruby that hung on a golden chain around her neck, the Princess wound it round the base of the Unicorn's horn. Placing her arms around his neck, she cried again because she loved him and she kissed him once again.

'Oh, Unicorn, my Unicorn, be safe, be free, remember me.'

Slowly he turned and walked away from her, away towards his mountain, his head held high, his horn rising up towards the morning sky, shining in the light. It shone so that even the trees he passed seemed to reflect the whiteness of the Unicorn.

Once he looked back. From the soft brownness of his eyes, the Princess could see that he loved her still, and would love her forever. At the base of his horn, her deep red ruby glowed against his whiteness.

Chapter 10

*A*lthough the way back through the forest seemed long to the Princess, it was still not fully daylight when she returned to the castle. The guards at the gates were still asleep and she reached her room unnoticed.

In her room, she lay fully dressed on her bed and fell immediately into a deep and dreamless sleep. She awoke refreshed and when her maid had dressed her in her wedding dress, she looked more beautiful than ever before.

It was a great day for Trevellia. Bells pealed, wine flowed, the sun shone and the people turned out in their hundreds to wish joy to the newly wedded Prince and Princess.

At the wedding party in the castle that evening,

the King drank from a cup made from the shining white Unicorn horn which he passed to Prince Tallyrand, the future King of Trevellia, so that the Prince also could drink.

And so, Prince Tallyrand and his Princess lived happily for many many long years. When the King of the land of Trevellia died, Prince Tallyrand succeeded to the throne and became as fair and just a ruler as his father-in-law before him.

The golden Princess, now Queen of Trevellia, bore her husband three sons and a daughter, and the land prospered under the rule of King Tallyrand and his Queen.

The Princess did not forget her Unicorn. Once a year, on the anniversary of her wedding eve, she would leave the castle early in the morning and ride alone into the forest. There, under the logwood trees, by the rushing, tumbling stream, the Unicorn would be waiting for her, magically white, with the ruby blazing from the base of his silver white horn.

No-one ever saw the Princess leave the castle and no-one saw her return.

Now, a very long time later, the land of Trevellia exists no more. Like so many other places, it has become part of one enormous country, marked on the map only by its river and the remains of the forest.

But the castle still stands. The gates of the castle and moat are still there and the river still flows by. In the castle, there is a tapestry showing the animals of the forest, the wild flowers and the magic Unicorn. On one of the walls a picture hangs. A picture that shows a Princess wearing a dress of emerald green, a rope of pearls around her neck, and with hair that gleams the colour of burnished gold flowing over her shoulders. In her hands

she holds a mirror of beaten silver which shows the reflection of a pure, milk white Unicorn who bears a horn shining silver white. The Unicorn rests his head on the lap of the Princess and his soft brown eyes reflect from the mirror with the great and endless love he has for the golden Princess.

The End